It's Groundhog Day, Dear Dragon

by Margaret Hillert
Illustrated by David Schimmell

NORWOOD HOUSE PRESS

DEAR CAREGIVER, The *Beginning-to-Read* series is a carefully written collection of classic readers you may remember from your own childhood. Each book features text comprised of common sight words to provide your child ample practice reading the words that appear most frequently in written text. The many additional details in the pictures enhance the story and offer the opportunity for you to help your child expand oral language and develop comprehension.

Begin by reading the story to your child, followed by letting him or her read familiar words and soon your child will be able to read the story independently. At each step of the way, be sure to praise your reader's efforts to build his or her confidence as an independent reader. Discuss the pictures and encourage your child to make connections between the story and his or her own life. At the end of the story, you will find reading activities and a word list that will help your child practice and strengthen beginning reading skills.

Above all, the most important part of the reading experience is to have fun and enjoy it!

Shannon Cannon

Shannon Cannon,
Literacy Consultant

Norwood House Press • P.O. Box 316598 • Chicago, Illinois 60631
For more information about Norwood House Press please visit our website at
www.norwoodhousepress.com or call 866-565-2900.

LIBRARY OF CONGRESS CATALOGING-IN-PUBLICATION DATA
   Hillert, Margaret.
    It's Groundhog Day, dear dragon / Margaret Hillert ; illustrated by David Schimmell.
      p. cm. -- (A beginning-to-read book)
    Summary: "A boy and his pet dragon go to see what will happen when the
groundhog peeks out of his hole"--Provided by publisher.
    ISBN-13: 978-1-59953-504-3 (library edition : alk. paper)
    ISBN-10: 1-59953-504-1 (library edition : alk. paper)
    ISBN-13: 978-1-60357-384-9 (e-book)
    ISBN-10: 1-60357-384-4 (e-book)
    [1. Groundhog Day--Fiction. 2. Dragons--Fiction.] I. Schimmell, David,
ill. II. Title. III. Title: It is Groundhog Day dear dragon.
    PZ7.H558Ish 2012
    [E]--dc23

                   2011038945
Manufactured in the United States of America in North Mankato, Minnesota
                 203R—052012

There is something I
want you to see.
Do you want to come
with me?

Yes, yes.
Where will we go, Father?
What will we see?

It is Groundhog Day.
The groundhog will
look for his shadow.

If he sees it, it will
stay cold for a little longer.
If he does not see it,
It will soon green up and be pretty.

That looks like the one
I play at school.

This one is big, big, big.

Oh, what a funny one it is.

But where is the groundhog?
What does he look like?
Oh, I see him! I see him!
He is brown and little.

He is all the way out!
What will he do now?

You guess he stays out, Father.
And I will guess he stays in.

He does not see his shadow.
He is out! He is out!

Now things will get green and pretty soon.

We can make Mother happy now.
We can get her something pretty.

What Father?
What?

No, no.
We can get Mother something
green and pretty now.

Look at this one——
and this——
and this——

Oh here is the one we want.
Mother will like this one.

Mother. Mother.
Look what we have for you.

I see.
I see.
It is green and pretty
and I like it.

Here I am with you.
You do not see your
shadow, dear dragon,
so it is a happy day.

READING REINFORCEMENT

The following activities support the findings of the National Reading Panel that determined the most effective components for reading instruction are: Phonemic Awareness, Phonics, Vocabulary, Fluency, and Text Comprehension.

Phonemic Awareness: The /ou/ sound

Sound Substitution: Say the words on the left to your child. Ask your child to repeat the word, changing the middle sound to the /**ou**/ sound.

moose = mouse	spat = spout	fund = found
grand = ground	catch = couch	shot = shout
pat = pout	load = loud	pond = pound
band = bound	horse= house	scoot = scout

Phonics: The letters o and u

1. Demonstrate how to form the letters **o** and **u** for your child.

2. Have your child practice writing **o** and **u** at least three times each.

3. Write down the following letters and spaces and ask your child to write the letters **o** and **u** on the spaces in each word:

gr_ _ nd	f_ _ nd	l_ _ d	c_ _ nt
s_ _ nd	_ _ t	m_ _ se	pr_ _ d
m_ _ th	fl_ _ r	r_ _ nd	h_ _ se

4. Ask your child to read each word.

Vocabulary: Contractions

1. Explain to your child that sometimes we combine two words to make one shorter word and that these new words are called contractions.

2. Point to the word It's on the front cover. Ask your child to name the two words that make It's. If your child doesn't know, explain that the word It's comes from the two words it and is.

3. Say the following contractions and ask your child to name the words that make each one:

don't	she's	can't	he'll	we've
I'll	doesn't	you're	isn't	they're

4. Write the following contractions and word pairs on separate pieces of paper.

did not / didn't	we will / we'll	are not / aren't
was not / wasn't	that is / that's	I am / I'm
we are / we're	you will / you'll	did not / didn't
you are / you're	let us / let's	it will / it'll

5. Ask your child to match the word pairs with the contractions they make.

Fluency: Choral Reading

1. Reread the story with your child at least two more times while your child tracks the print by running a finger under the words as they are read. Ask your child to read the words he or she knows with you.

2. Reread the story aloud together. Be careful to read at a rate that your child can keep up with.

3. Repeat choral reading and allow your child to be the lead reader and ask him or her to change from a whisper to a loud voice while you follow along and change your voice.

Text Comprehension: Discussion Time

1. Ask your child to retell the sequence of events in the story.

2. To check comprehension, ask your child the following questions:

   • Why are all the people gathered together outside?

   • What is supposed to happen if the groundhog sees his shadow?

   • What is supposed to happen if the groundhog doesn't see his shadow?

   • Do you think that the groundhog can really let us know how long cold weather will last?

***It's Groundhog Day, Dear Dragon* uses the 77 words listed below.**
This list can be used to practice reading the words that appear in the text.
You may wish to write the words on index cards and use them to help your
child build automatic word recognition. Regular practice with these words
will enhance your child's fluency in reading connected text.

a	dragon	his	now	there
all				things
am	Father	I	oh	this
and	for	if	one	to
at	fun	in	out	
	funny	is		up
be		it	play	
big	get		pretty	want
brown	go	like		way
but	green	little	school	we
	groundhog	longer	see(s)	what
can	guess	look(s)	shadow	where
cold			so	will
come	happy	make	something	with
	have	me	soon	
day	he	Mother	stay(s)	yes
dear	her			you
do	here	no	that	your
does	him	not	the	

ABOUT THE AUTHOR Margaret Hillert has written over 80 books for
children who are just learning to read. Her books
have been translated into many different languages and over a million children
throughout the world have read her books. She first started writing poetry as
a child and has continued to write for children and adults throughout her life. A
first grade teacher for 34 years, Margaret is now retired from teaching and lives in
Michigan where she likes to write, take walks in the morning, and care for her three cats.

Photograph by Glenna Washburn

ABOUT THE ADVISER Shannon Cannon contributed the activities pages that appear in
this book. Shannon serves as a literacy consultant and provides
staff development to help improve reading instruction. She is a frequent presenter at educational
conferences and workshops. Prior to this she worked as an elementary school teacher and as
president of a curriculum publishing company.